ALL MY HORSES

STORY BY **ALEXIS STEINER** • PICTURES BY **WILHELM JARUSKA** • **LERNER** PUBLICATIONS COMPANY, MINNEAPOLIS

AN OUTSTANDING SELECTION FROM *Austria*

First published in the United States of America 1965 by

Lerner Publications Company, Minneapolis, Minnesota.

Library of Congress Catalog Card Number: 64-8402.

Originally published in Austria under the title *Alle meine Pferde,*

© 1963 by Verlag für Jugend und Volk, Vienna.

Translation by Vera Lieban. This edition © 1965 by

Lerner Publications Company. Printed in U. S. A.

INTRODUCTION

My profession is such that I have had a great deal of experience with horses, and I can truly say that this has been a very satisfying kind of work.

The few introductory words to this book are said out of my deeply felt love of horses. Luckily there are still many horse lovers, but only a few of these people ask themselves, "What is the future of the horse?" The thoroughbred is the center of attention today, and horse racing in the last few years has developed considerably in many countries, but the good old everyday workhorse, that has faithfully served mankind for several thousand years, seems to have no more place in the world of airplanes and space travel, and especially of autos and tractors. The workhorse is being forgotten.

Therefore, it is especially gratifying that there are some artists who have the taste and talent to present in simple, moving words and through the language of pictures in an imaginative and effective fashion, the problem of "All My Horses" to young people—and, perhaps, to their elders, too.

Dr. H. Lehrner
Director, Department of Animal Husbandry,
Vienna, Austria

Martin and Larissa
bring ice to the city
from the ice factory.
They have made this trip for many years.
The wagon load is heavy, and the street
is hard. Larissa is carrying a colt in her
belly, and this is the reason Martin is
walking beside her. He is leading his
horse very carefully by her bridle. The
sun is rising over the houses. The early
morning train is now leaving the railroad
station. A bakery truck rattles down the
street, with a milk wagon following behind.
A black auto hurries by into the alley.

Martin wants to sell his ice.
The butcher, called "Soupbone", takes three blocks.
A car and a truck pass by.
Larissa and Martin continue;
up the street, down the street, over the hard pavement.
Lines of automobiles are parked along the curbs. They
are still asleep. The innkeeper of the "Golden Ox" on
4th Street bought nothing. He said, "We now have
a refrigerator." The Hotel Crown has also used
refrigeration for a long time. Manfred, the candymaker
on 11th Street, bought twelve blocks of ice.
Then he said, "This dozen must last until Monday.
Then I will begin to use an electric refrigerator.
It's about time! Now move on with your wagon so I
can move my car in front of the door."

The journey continues.
Twenty, thirty, forty streets and
only a few people buy ice.
Even Heinz's Delicatessen bought nothing.
Heinz's Delicatessen, too, now has electrical
refrigeration. And he was Martin's best customer.

When the sun was shining down from directly overhead,
Martin had sold only half of his ice.
Larissa went slowly, very slowly, through the streets.
It seems that all the automobiles in the city are on the
streets, and the avenues, and the boulevards.
They roar and screech from all directions.

"They sneak up like a pack of wolves," said Martin to Larissa.
"What will happen when your little colt is born?
How will it be able to run along at your side?
There is hardly any room left for you on the streets.
Be careful, we are coming near the intersection.
Stop, Larissa, stop!"
The traffic light turned red and
Martin tugged on the reins.
Larissa stood still with Martin next to her.
It seemed as if they were in a sea of automobiles.

The sun in the sky was shining brightly,
and the automobile drivers were happy.
Then streams of water began to trickle
into the street from Martin's wagon.
Martin didn't even notice.
He stared at the red light and thought:
What will happen to you and me, and
your colt, Larissa? He leaned his head
against Larissa's neck, and he patted her
mane with his hand.

"Hey, Old Man," one of the drivers suddenly shouted.
"What are you doing here?
Your ice is melting, so you better go home."
Martin was startled. Water was running in all
directions from his wagon. The light changed to yellow,
then green, and Martin loosened the reins.

Larissa moved on,
but just then another car cut in
front of her. The auto stopped suddenly,
and its wheels screeched.
She reared up in fright. But Martin
held Larissa tightly by the reins.
Then the driver shouted:
"Pay more attention, Old Man!
One foot more, and this would have been
the last trip for you and your horse!"
"What about you," Martin called back.
"Haven't you any eyes in your head?
Why did you cross over in front of me?
Can't you see that my mare is carrying
a foal in her belly?
Just look how she is trembling!"

He turned to Larissa and said tenderly,
"My good horse," and patted her gently.
"Calm down, I am right next to you, calm down . . .
there, there, be good . . ."
Larissa slowly stopped trembling.
After a short while she put her head on Martin's shoulder.

It was evening
when Martin and Larissa returned home.
The sun had already set.

"Oh, but you were in a hurry to get home, Larissa!
You were certainly anxious to bring your colt into
the world!" Martin said with excitement.

He kneeled down on the straw in front of Larissa's
newborn colt, and held a clean white cloth in his hands.
Larissa whinnied softly.
She lowered her head to lick her young one.
"Yes, welcome it, welcome it! That's right,
that's the way to do it, lick your wet baby pony dry.
This way it will dry, and then warm up.
Soon it will be able to stand up and nurse.
Come, let me help you.
Don't be frightened, I won't hurt him."
Martin kept talking softly to the mare,
and with the white cloth dried the colt.

Gently, very gently, Larissa's tongue glided
over the shiny fur of her young colt,
over the slender back, over the thin hips,
over the neck, over the head.
Over and over, tirelessly . . . .

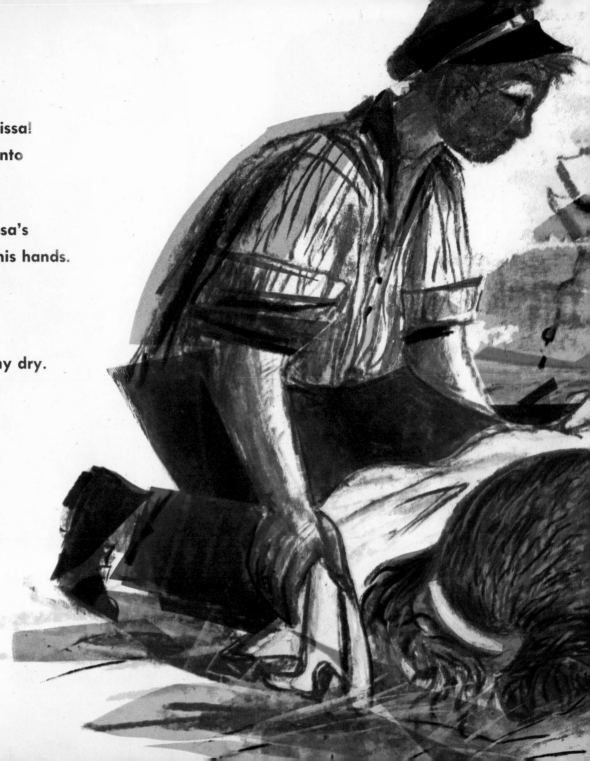

And how did the colt feel?

Half asleep he stretched out his forelegs.

Then his hind legs, too.

After that he turned from his side to his stomach
and lifted his head up.

Oh, what a heavy head he has!

And then the young colt raised himself up to
his full height.

That wasn't easy for him to do.

His thin legs wavered . . .

The little horse swayed like a blade of grass
in the wind.

Larissa, however, waited patiently,
until the little one stood by her side
and reached over to nurse.

"Drink, drink, my little horse," said Martin.
"I'm so happy that everything went well."
Then he sat down, and stretched out his legs,
for he was very tired.
He rested himself comfortably.

"Oh how beautiful your little colt is!
Someday he will be a fine draft horse."

Then he continued:
"When I was putting the wagon away, like
I do every day,
the manager of the ice factory started to
talk to me again.
"Martin," he said,
"Get rid of your horse and wagon.
The time it takes you to make one trip
through town, our trucks make ten trips.
How can you make a living, when day
after day half of your ice melts.
Come to work for us, now that
you've gotten old.
I have a nice job for you.
You can work on the ice trucks."

"Did you hear that, Larissa? They want me
to work on the trucks.

"No," I said, "I can't do that," and I came
right back to you.

"In the meantime you had brought your little
pony into the world.
Look how he stands! It's pure joy to watch him."

The little colt drank its fill.
Now he wanted to sleep and laid down in the straw.
Larissa remained standing over him so she could
give the colt her milk when he would awaken hungry.
"Where do you get your strength, after such a day?
What a good mother you are, Larissa," said Martin.

"But I shouldn't be too surprised because all
the mares that I used to have before
you were good mothers, too.
Forty years ago
I moved here from my village in the mountains.
That was the time when your grandmother,
Senta, pulled my wagon. Your mother, Lena,
came into the world in this very stall.
I, myself, rubbed her down until she was
dry and stood up on her little legs.
She was a truly beautiful colt.

People enjoyed watching as we drove
through the city,
Senta and the graceful Lena at her side.
And you too, Larissa, a few years later."
Then Martin became silent, and bent his head.

After a little while he continued sadly:
"But now, Larissa, now all is over.
We won't go to the city anymore.
The city no longer has place for us.
She no longer has any place for our colt.
Your young one can't come along to town,
and yet, there must be a solution,
and I must find it."

Larissa looked over to Martin.
Her eyes were dark and deep. She listened.
Her fine, slender ears perked forward.
"Yes, Larissa, I must find it,"
Martin murmured more softly than before.
"And I will find it."
The last words could hardly be heard.
Martin quietly fell asleep.

Then the colt woke up.
It stood up on its legs faster than before,
and Larissa nursed it.
Later, after it had its fill and nestled into
the straw, Larissa also laid down.
A tiny flame flickered in the barn lantern for
only a little while longer.
As it died out, a low murmur was heard between
Larissa and her colt.

"Listen to me," Larissa whispered to her colt:
"Martin, the old man next to us, is
a good human being.
I have been with him ever since I was born.
I work for him, and he gives you and me shelter,
he cares for us and he provides food for us.
There have always been some good people among
men. We horses have lived among human
beings since ancient times.
Today Martin doesn't know how we can continue
working and living together.
I don't know either. But I want to tell you how
it all happened to come about:

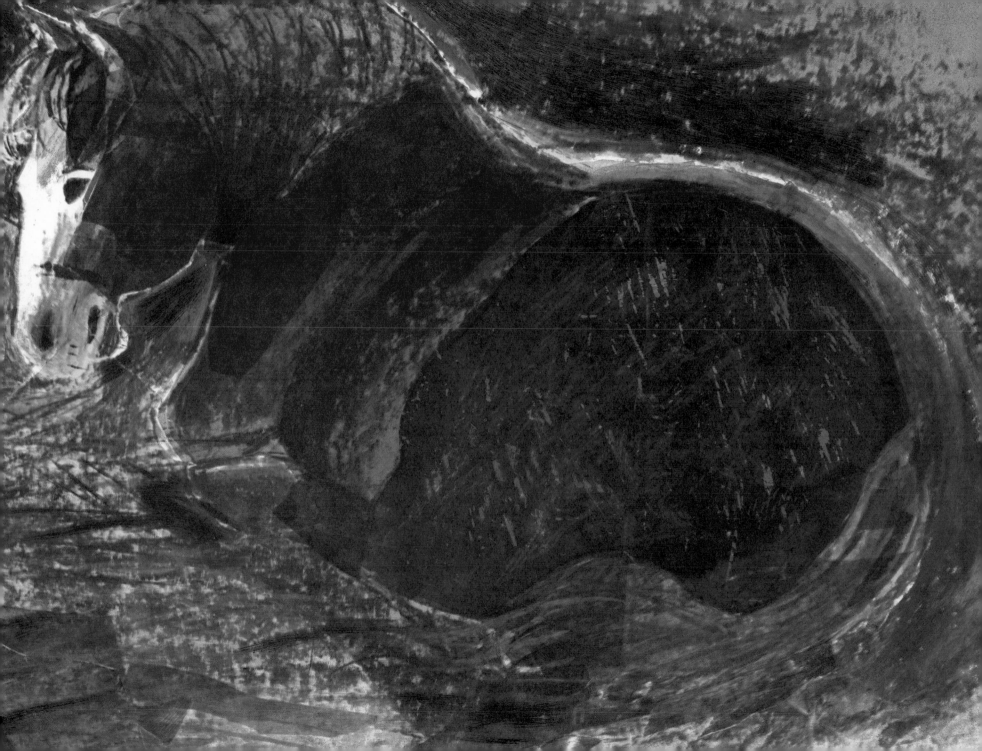

In the beginning we horses were
free and lived on the
broad areas of the plains.

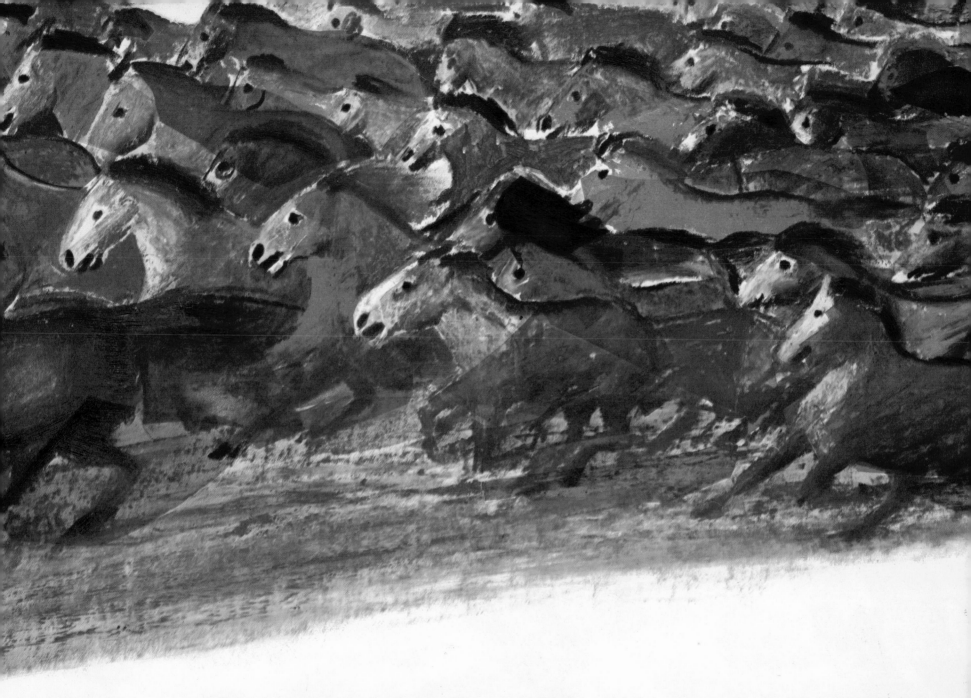

How wonderful it was to gallop along with the herd. A stallion would lead us and the mares and colts followed behind him.

It was hard when winter came. Food was difficult to find.
Wolves, and other wild creatures among the animals, would attack us.

Then man came.

He is smaller, but much more intelligent than we are.

He captured and tamed us.

We became his fellow laborer and did every kind of work.

Man harnessed us to the plow and to the wagon,

and we pulled them.

Our freedom was gone,

but we lived in safety.

He gave us food even during the winter.

He gave us shelter.

He protected us against wolves and

other wild animals.

And he helped us raise our young.

Men have again and again made war
among themselves.
This caused them much suffering. We suffered
greatly, too, because we had to join in their
battles. At first they harnessed us to
their war chariots.
Then they began to ride on us.
We resisted this, but they still remained
saddled on our backs.
They hammered iron to our hoofs to help
us bear the stony roads.

Entire armies rode mounted on us.
We carried them over the whole world.

There was a time when men dressed themselves, and their strongest war-horses, in armor, in order that we should all be protected in battle. A king would ride with a hundred mounted armor-clad knights to meet his queen.

We also pulled the golden coaches of emperors.

Man needed us for almost everything.
With our four legs under man's saddle
he became faster than cattle and deer,
faster than the fox,
the rabbit, and the dog.
We pulled his wagons over mountains.
We dragged his hay into barns.

We towed men's boats up rivers.

The coachman's horn would sound merrily as he drove his stagecoach through the countryside.

Man took us across oceans and brought us to countries
where we had never been before.

Man built great cities, and we were part of them. He rode on us over their streets and boulevards.

We pulled the milk-wagons, the bread-wagons, the brick-wagons . . . and the ice-wagons, too.

We drove people on their holidays,
and we also pulled their funeral wagons to the cemetery.

One day, however, man invented carriages that could
move by themselves, the locomotive and the automobile.
The locomotive rode on iron rails and pulled a whole
train of railroad cars over mountains and valleys.
The automobile travelled freely on the street,
but it needed a smooth, hard road.
Neither of them needed horses.
A hard road was not good for us.
It hurt our legs.
But the automobile drove easily on such roads.
It soon drove faster, much faster, than we could run.

Now men let us trot and gallop a little at racetracks on the outskirts of the city.

Now men let us dance and play a little,
at the riding school, and the circus.
But only a very few of us can do this.
Only certain exceptional horses can perform
in these places.
Workhorses like us are not needed there.

Today the city has no more place for horses.
Automobiles fill the streets.
They descend upon us from all sides,
just as the wolves once did.
They crowd all the boulevards,
the roadways, and the squares.
The people of the city don't need us anymore.
They are getting rid of us."

A light shone brightly through the barn window.
The whispering between Larissa and her colt stopped.
Larissa stood up.
Her little one also rose quickly to its feet.
Martin awoke.

"Oh, my," he yawned half asleep, and said:
"I fell asleep, last night, instead of
watching over you."
He reached for the lantern, placed a new candle
inside, and lit it.
He saw Larissa and the colt.
The colt nursed,
and Larissa picked hay from the manger.
"Oh, up so soon," Martin called out happily.
"One can see at a glance how beautiful
your colt is, Larissa.
Healthy and peppy, too!
He is pure joy to look at."

Martin patted the colt on the neck,
but then stopped suddenly.
"Pure joy," he said sadly,
and laid his head on Larissa's neck.
"But what shall we do with our joy?
Where shall we go?"
Martin pondered.
His hands stroked the mane of the colt.

Only after a long while did Martin lift his
head and say:
"We must go back, Larissa!
We will return to the mountains, to our homeland,
to our old village.
There we are still needed."
Martin brought some fresh hay to Larissa's manger
and added some oats and water.
Thoughtfully he blew out the lantern.
Then he walked over to his little house.
As he stepped out again he carefully closed the
door behind him.
A knapsack hung from his shoulders.
He led Larissa out of the stable.
The colt tripped after them.
Now Martin closed the stable door and the gate to
the yard.
A man, a mare and a colt stood on the street.
They are moving to a place where man and
horse still need each other.